SUPER SOCCER BOY

SUPER SOCCER BOY

ATTACK OF THE GIANT SLUGS

BY JUDY BROWN

Piccadilly Press

For Dad

First published in Great Britain in 2010 by
Piccadilly Press, a Templar/Bonnier publishing company
Deepdene Lodge, Deepdene Avenue, Dorking, Surrey RH5 4AT
www.piccadillypress.co.uk

ISBN: 978 1 84812 098 3

3 5 7 9 10 8 6 4

Printed and bound by
CPI Group (UK) Ltd, Croydon, CR0 4YY
Cover design by Simon Davis
Cover illustration by Judy Brown
Text design by Simon Davis

Mixed Sources
Product group from well-managed
forests and other controlled sources
www.fsc.org Cert no. TT-COC-002227
© 1996 Forest Stewardship Council
FSC

Chapter One

Granddad Gribble

It was a Saturday morning in early September and as usual Harry Gribble, also known as Super Soccer Boy, was playing for his Little League team in the local park.

'Great goal, Harry!' shouted his granddad from the touchline.

Since Harry had been transformed by a bolt of lightning from 'Harry Gribble who couldn't even dribble' into Super Soccer Boy, his granddad really looked forward to the Saturday morning games. It hadn't been long ago that Granddad had thought that Harry couldn't kick his way out of a wet paper bag. Things were very different now.

Peeeep! The final whistle blew.

'Twelve-nil, Harry,' said Granddad. 'Great result!'

Of course, Harry's team could have won by much more, but Harry didn't try too hard – that wouldn't be fair. And he didn't want everyone to think he was hogging the ball – football is a team game after all!

'Are you coming to help out at the allotment this afternoon?' asked Granddad.

'Yep! Just need to go home and change out of my football stuff first. Sorry I haven't helped out much this year – football's taken up all my time,' said Harry.

Harry's granddad was a keen gardener. He was a good one, too. He was as mad about gardening as Harry was about football, and that was saying something. For the last three years, he'd won first prize in the Middletown and District Giant Vegetable Competition (Marrow Section).

'How are the marrows coming along?' asked Harry, as they walked back to his house.

Harry wasn't particularly keen on gardening, but he liked spending time with his granddad. Granddad knew loads about football and had

played quite a lot when he was younger. He knew all about the old star players and Harry loved listening to him talk about them. Besides, Granddad had taken him for a big pig-out at the burger bar after he'd won the first prize yet again last year, to thank Harry for his help at the allotment.

'Best year yet, I think,' said Granddad proudly. 'You'll be able to see for yourself. We can make some sandwiches to eat up at the allotment – a gardeners' picnic.'

'When's the competition?'

'Three weeks tomorrow,' Granddad said. 'I've been feeding my veggies on my special organic formula. They'll be even more lovely and plump by then. And it's not just the marrows either! I wouldn't be surprised if I won the prize for biggest tomatoes and biggest cabbage too, this year.' He stared dreamily into the distance. 'Maybe I'll even win Best in Show.'

'Wow!' said Harry. What else could he say?

Harry's stomach rumbled expectantly as he remembered last year's burger treat. When they arrived back at Harry's house in Crumbly Drive, his mum was waiting for them.

'Good game this morning?' she asked.

'Brilliant!' said Granddad. 'Harry was on great form. Mind you, these days he always is!'

'What do you want in your sandwich?' Mum called to Harry as he dashed upstairs to change into his gardening clothes.

'I'll have whatever Granddad's having,' replied Harry, feeling adventurous. Granddad's taste in sandwich fillings was a bit experimental.

A few minutes later, Harry was in the kitchen with Ron, his pet rat, sitting on his shoulder.

'Don't forget to pack something for Ron,' he said.

'That's your job,' said Mum, as she finished making the gardeners' picnic and Granddad made a flask of tea.

'Can I come tooooo?' asked Harry's little sister, Daisy.

Harry winced.

'Not this time, poppet,' said Granddad. 'We're going to be a bit busy.'

Harry knew he was thinking about the last time Daisy 'helped out' – too young to tell which was which, she had pulled up all Granddad's seedlings and left the weeds to grow!

'Phew!' said Harry quietly.

Chapter Two

The First Attack

The allotments, where Harry's granddad grew his vegetables, backed onto the school playing fields. In fact, every now and then a stray football ended up among them, usually because Harry had kicked it too hard.

As allotments go it was quite a big one. There were thirty strips of land altogether, each one about ten metres wide and twenty metres long. They weren't separated by fences because every gardener knew their own boundary. Some had a little shed or greenhouse and some had both. There was a seed store and a small shop, which sold gardening supplies, that was only open at the weekend. It was a nice friendly place to pass the time and grow some juicy vegetables.

'Poo!' said Harry as they approached the gate. 'What is that pong?!'

'Someone must have had some manure delivered,' Granddad replied. 'Funny time of year for it, though.'

When they walked through the gates of the allotments, Harry's granddad stopped dead. The colour drained from his face and a look of horror came over it.

'Oh no!' he moaned.

'What is it, Granddad?'

Harry had never seen his granddad look like that before and he was worried.

'My vegetables!' Granddad pointed a shaky finger towards his allotment. It was a wreck.

'What's happened?' said Harry, shocked at the sight.

'My vegetables!' gasped Granddad.

'Granddad?' said Harry.

'My vegetables!' Granddad gasped again.

Harry took his granddad gently by the hand and walked him towards the allotment. It was not a pretty sight.

'My vegetables!'

Harry tried to imagine how he would feel if someone came into his room and trashed all his

football programmes. A shiver went down his spine.

Granddad spoke again. 'Slugs,' he said grimly.

Harry looked down at the wrecked plants. 'D'you think so, Granddad? Could they really make this much mess?' It looked to Harry more like a couple of elephants had been ballroom dancing through his granddad's vegetables.

Granddad pointed to a half-eaten cucumber that lay on the ground. Yes, it looked like it was covered in slug slime. But they must have been pretty big slugs to have produced that much slime. It was strange, too, but it didn't look like they'd done much damage on any of the other allotments.

Harry bent down to take a closer look.

'Poo!' he said. 'This is what smells.' He picked up the remains of the cucumber then dropped it almost instantly. 'Ow! That stings.'

'What does?' said Granddad. It sounded like he was at last returning to the real world after the nasty shock.

'The slime. Poo! Now my hand stinks too,' Harry said, wiping it on his trousers.

'That's odd. Never known slug slime that stings before.' Granddad looked really sad.

'Right!' said Harry decisively. He grabbed a garden chair from inside the shed and sat his granddad down. 'I'll clear some of this mess up. It might not be as bad as it looks.' He was trying to sound positive but he thought it probably was as bad as it looked.

Harry put on Granddad's gardening gloves and zoomed around the allotment at super speed, throwing and booting the spoiled plants and veg with perfect accuracy into a big pile. Then he straightened up the bamboo growing-poles and set the pots upright.

'There,' he said when he'd finished. Surprisingly, it really wasn't as bad as he'd first thought. There were even a few vegetables that had been left untouched – but the big ones were mush. The prize marrows were nowhere to be seen.

Suddenly, Granddad jumped up. 'The greenhouse!' he said. 'I moved my biggest marrows to the greenhouse because it was chilly last night.' He ran over and slid the door open. 'Thank goodness!'

There in the greenhouse, safe and sound, were four of the biggest marrows Harry had ever seen. The largest was the size of a pot-bellied pig.

'Wow!' said Harry, amazed. 'Awesome marrows, Granddad!'

Chapter Three

Slug Suspicions

Granddad rushed over to his biggest marrow and hugged it.

'Margaret!' he said, smothering it in kisses.

'Margaret?!' Harry repeated.

'Oh, they've all got names, Harry. This one's Margaret, that's Mary, the one at the back is Marie and the little one here is Mabel.'

My granddad is insane, thought Harry. He'd

forgotten that Granddad always gave his biggest vegetables names. Granddad was one of those gardeners who liked talking to their plants and names made them even more personal.

'Oh, my lovely marrows, you're safe! Don't you worry, Daddy will look after you. I'll not let those nasty slugs get you – no I won't.'

Harry suddenly became aware that they were not alone. With the same skill he used on pitch

MARGARET!

to tell where players were positioned even if he couldn't actually see them, he knew someone was watching them from the far side of the allotments. He turned and, out of the corner of his eye, just managed to glimpse someone in a shed. But whoever it was dived for cover before he had a chance to see them properly. As far as Harry could make out, the slug trails came from the same direction – and the revolting smell, too.

'Granddad, whose allotment is that over there?' asked Harry, pointing to the shed where he'd seen the shadowy figure moments before.

Granddad, who was still lovingly patting Margaret the marrow, looked up. 'Erm . . . that's Miss Bunsen's. Why?'

'Do you know her?'

'Oh yes – a fellow giant vegetable grower.

She's a charming old dear. Been here for years. She used to be a teacher at the secondary school. Biology, I think.'

'Oh yes – I know her too,' said Harry. 'She came and talked to us when we started the school Gardening Club. She's potty about animals as well.'

'Why do you ask?' said Granddad.

'Oh, it's probably nothing. It's just I think she was watching us.'

'Really?' But Granddad wasn't interested and had started weeding.

Harry tried to use his super vision to see through the window of Miss Bunsen's shed, but it was too dark inside.

'Granddad?'

'Yes, Harry.'

'Don't you use slug pellets to stop the slugs from eating your plants?'

'Yes, the safe organic ones — the ones that are OK if Daisy and Ron are around and eat them by mistake.'

'So if there were slugs, why didn't the pellets work? There were none left when I cleared up.'

Granddad looked up from his weeding. 'Yes, that is a bit odd. They've always worked before and it didn't rain yesterday, which might have washed them away . . .' He scratched his head. 'Let's have a cup of tea — I'm parched.'

They sat with their tea and sandwiches while Ron helped himself to some of the ruined veg that didn't have slug slime on it.

'I'm going to come back here tonight after dinner and guard my marrows. And I'm bringing salt with me,' said Granddad.

'Salt?' said Harry.

'You must have seen what happens if you put salt on a slug, Harry.'

'Can't say I have,' Harry replied. 'Hmmm – you young people know nothing! Too much time wasted playing video games. If all else fails, you can sprinkle slugs with salt to get rid of them. Not too much though mind – it's bad for the soil.'

'I'll bear that in mind,' said Harry making a mental note to look it up on YouTube later on.

'Anyway, no slug is going to get these beauties,' said Granddad, giving his marrows one more pat.

Chapter Four

Dotty

In the foul-smelling shed on the other side of the allotments, Miss Dorothy Bunsen – Dotty to her friends – was hopping mad.

'Blast it! You didn't go into the greenhouse!' she said, looking into the specially-constructed cage in the darkest corner of her shed. Inside were ten rather large black slugs, glistening in the semi-dark. Each was the size of a big fat cat. They turned to look at her.

'I should have trained you to open the door. Those massive marrows are still safe. I have to make sure they're ruined before it's too late!'

Miss Bunsen's eyes glazed over as she stared at the shiny black creatures.

EVER SINCE SHE RETIRED FROM TEACHING, SIX YEARS AGO, MISS BUNSEN HAD SPENT MOST OF HER TIME EITHER HELPING OUT AT THE ANIMAL RESCUE CENTRE OR GARDENING.

OH YOU POOR WEE THING.

I'LL MAKE IT ALL BETTER.

OH YOU POOR WEE THING.

YOU NEED SOME WATER.

SHE'D ALWAYS LOVED GROWING THINGS, BUT WHEN SHE WAS A SCIENCE TEACHER, SHE'D NEVER HAD ENOUGH TIME TO SPEND ON GARDENING. EVERY YEAR THOUGH, SHE WENT TO THE MIDDLETOWN VEGETABLE SHOW.

LOOK AT THAT BEAUTIFUL ONION!

1st

MIDDLETOWN 2000

BEST IN SHOW

AND WHEN SHE RETIRED AT LAST, SHE DREAMED OF WINNING A TROPHY FOR HERSELF!

LAST YEAR WHEN HARRY'S GRANDDAD WON YET AGAIN, MISS BUNSEN COULD NO LONGER CONTAIN HER **ANGER!!!**

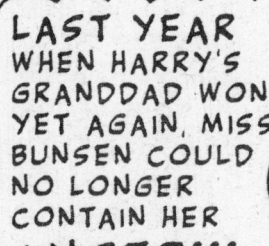

NOT AGAIN! THAT TERRY GRIBBLE NEEDS TEACHING A LESSON.

SHE DECIDED TO CHANGE HER TACTICS...

JUST BY CHANCE, ONE DAY SHE FOUND HER SHED WAS FULL OF SLUGS. THEY'D SQUEEZED THROUGH A KNOTHOLE TO GET TO HER SEED POTATOES, BUT THEY'D EATEN SOMETHING ELSE AS WELL, MISS BUNSEN'S **SUPER-GROW!**

SO THAT'S WHY YOU'RE STILL IN HERE, YOU'VE GROWN TOO BIG TO GET BACK THROUGH THE HOLE! FASCINATING.

29

Miss Bunsen spoke again to her mutated slugs.

'I think we need to make you just a tiny bit bigger, so you can slide open that door,' she said with an evil grin. She carried over a crate of late-season mushy strawberries that she'd got cheap from the greengrocer and sprinkled their usual dose – a teaspoonful – of Super-Grow compound on top.

Then Miss Bunsen poured the strawberries into the cage.

Slurp! Squelch! Gobble!

The strawberries were gone in seconds!

'That's right – eat them all up, my dears. You've got a busy night ahead of you.'

The slugs were already beginning to grow.

Chapter Five

Mutant Slug Attacks

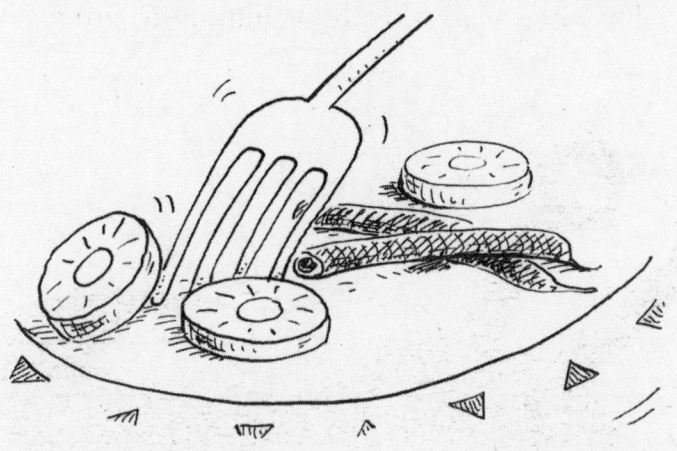

Harry had just eaten his dinner. Well, most of it. He was still pushing the last of his vegetables around the plate – some beans and carrots from Granddad's allotment.

'Mum,' he asked, 'is it OK if I go back to the allotment after dinner to see how Granddad's getting on?'

He had told her about the ruined veggies they'd found and about Granddad's plan for a stakeout.

'If you finish all your vegetables, Harry. I keep telling you, you need —'

'Yes, I know, my five-a-day.'

YUK, CARROTS.

'Not going out to play football then?'

'I think Granddad might need my help,' said Harry.

'All right,' said Mum, 'but be careful. Take your phone and your torch – it gets very dark down there at night.'

'I'll take Ron, too,' said Harry, scooping him up and putting him in his hoody.

Harry cycled to the allotments to join Granddad on his slug stakeout. As he got closer, the foul smell seemed even stronger than before. Ron looked as though he was going to throw up.

'Poo! Smells like Dad the morning after a curry!' said Harry. He leaned his bike against the fence, took out his torch and went to find his granddad.

As he walked, Harry shone the torch in front of him to light his path. Harry's super soccer skills made him aware of even the slightest movement, and he spotted something up ahead, by Granddad's allotment.

'Probably a fox,' he said to Ron. 'Keep your head down.' He aimed his torch at whatever it was, and caught a glimpse of a large black shape, slinking off into the shadows. Definitely not a fox.

'Blimey, Ron. What on earth was that?'

Harry shone the torch around Granddad's allotment and what he saw took his breath away.

Huge black slugs were munching away at the rest of vegetables. They turned towards him and Harry could have sworn that they were glaring. Then, going a hundred times faster than you've ever seen a slug go, they disappeared.

Harry saw one more at the door of Granddad's

greenhouse. He sped over and did a giant goalkeeper's leap, landing just a metre away from the slug. It squelched off, startled.

'Granddad! Granddad!' shouted Harry. He'd just realised that Granddad was sitting outside his shed, dozing. *It's a good job he's never been a security guard,* thought Harry. 'What?! What's going on?' said Granddad, waking up with a jolt.

Harry appeared by his side.

'Oh, Harry, it's you. I must have dropped off.'

'You wouldn't believe what I just saw,' said Harry. 'This allotment was full of massive slugs. They were everywhere!'

Granddad switched on his own torch and pointed it at the greenhouse. The door was slightly open and there was a pool of stinky slime in front of it. It looked like Harry had frightened the slug off just in time.

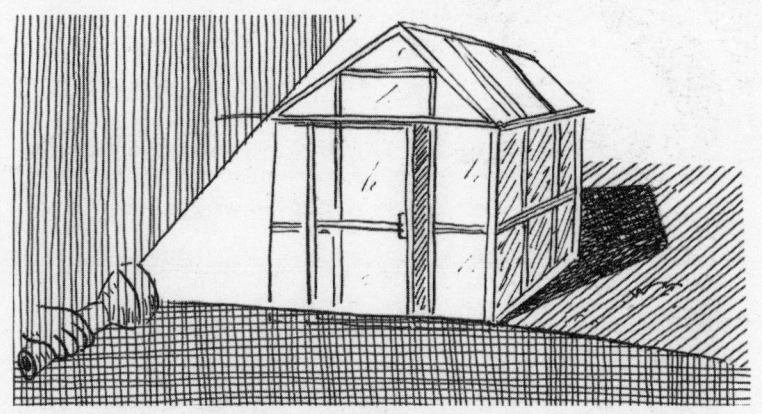

'Look! They've tried to get into the greenhouse!' said Granddad.

'You should have seen how fast they moved,' Harry said. 'I wonder where they went.'

The smell from the slime was still very strong and some of the blobs were smoking slightly, scorching patches of grass. Harry suddenly had a disturbing thought: What if the slugs got onto the football pitch? There weren't any vegetables there but even if they just went across the grass it would be ruined! As Harry looked at the half-eaten vegetables on Granddad's allotment he wondered again why the slugs didn't seem to

have damaged the other allotments.

'Blow me down!' said Granddad. 'What a mess! Still, at least Margaret and the others are safe. Let's make sure nothing can get into this greenhouse, and then we should go home. We can come back tomorrow and tidy up – it's too dark to do anything now.'

'OK,' agreed Harry.

They tied the handle of the door up with some garden twine from the shed and went home.

The slugs hated light, so when Harry had started flashing his torch around, they had returned to the safety of their cage through the secret door in the back of Miss Bunsen's shed. When they got there, Miss Bunsen was far from happy.

'You stupid creatures!' she yelled. 'You were supposed to get into that greenhouse while the old man was asleep, not just slime around gorging yourselves.'

I'LL GET THOSE MARROWS!!!

She glared at them, and if it weren't for the fact that she knew they were only slugs, she could have sworn that they glared back.

'No food for you tonight, you naughty things – you've had quite enough already.'

Miss Bunsen peered out of the window and watched as Harry and his granddad secured the greenhouse and headed off home.

'I'll get your precious marrows tomorrow, you'll see,' she snarled after them.

Chapter Six

Freedom for Slugs

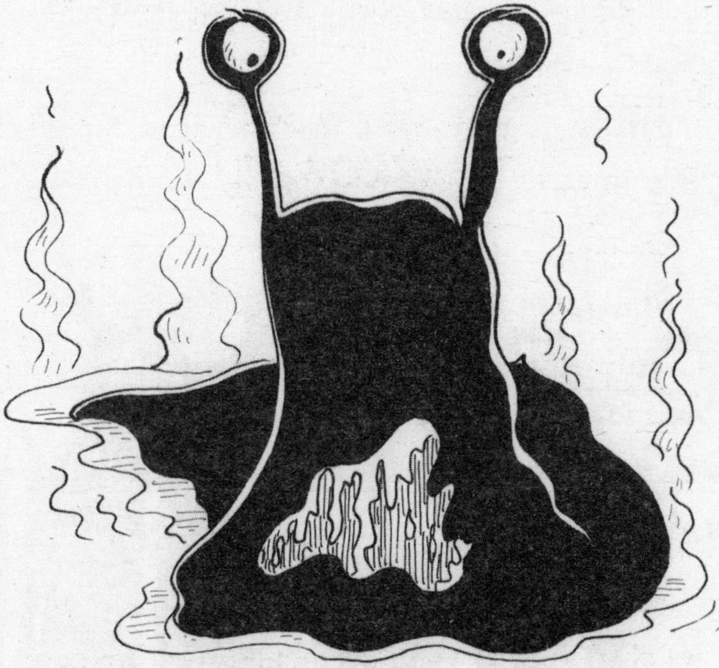

While all the human beings were safely tucked up in bed, the slugs in the shed began to get restless.

One problem was that the bigger the slugs got, the more crowded their cage became and, even though Miss Bunsen had extended it several times to make it more comfortable for them, it was a very tight squeeze. The other problem was that the bigger they got, the bigger their brains became. They were beginning to think for themselves.

The slugs were cross that they had missed Miss Bunsen's nightly feed and their usual dose

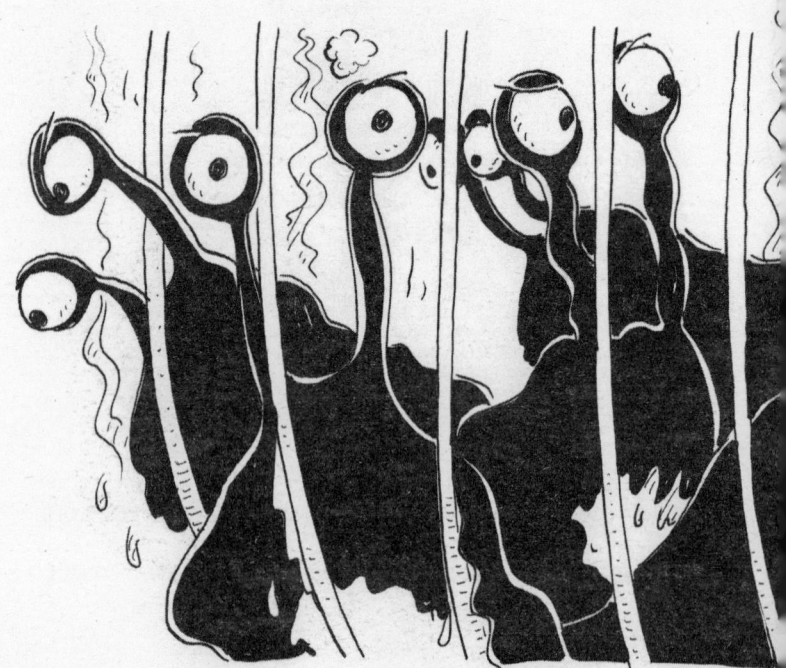

of Super-Grow compound. They started pushing and shoving against each other in the rather cramped cage. They pushed so hard that the cage door began to bulge outwards. It wasn't long before it gave way completely.

The slugs poured out of the cage in search of food, and the first thing they saw was Miss Bunsen's Super-Grow compound. The biggest slug slimed over to the container and knocked it down to get the lid off.

The slugs scoffed the lot!

And then things really started to change.

As the massive overdose of Super-Grow hit their systems, the slugs were completely transformed – and they now had a plan of their own!

The biggest slug stood in front of the others and they all watched him, swaying together from side to side.

(For the purposes of this book, the slugs' thoughts have been translated from the original 'slugish' into English.)

47

The slugs swayed together as one. They couldn't speak because they have no vocal cords, but it was as if they had some psychic link – what one slug thought, they all thought. And what they were thinking now was, ESCAPE!

So that's what they did.

All together, they pushed at the side of the shed. They were so big now that their combined weight began to splinter the wood. They pushed and pushed until – *CRUNCH* – the whole side of the shed broke away.

The slugs were free! And they were still growing . . .

Chapter Seven

Sluggish Dreams

Back in his room in Crumbly Drive, Harry was having a restless night. It was filled with nightmares about giant slugs sliming all over the place, ruining football pitches, parks, gardens – in fact anything they came into contact with. The slugs he dreamed about were much bigger than the ones he'd seen and they actually had a plan: to destroy the people who were always trying to destroy them.

The first thing Harry did when he woke up the following morning was to ring his granddad.

'I think we should go back and find those slugs tonight, Granddad,' he said. 'I've a feeling there could be serious trouble if we don't.'

'OK, Harry, but what will we do with them if we catch them?' asked Granddad.

'Hmm, I'm not quite sure yet,' said Harry, 'but I'm working on it.'

The second thing Harry did was to ring his best mate, Jake.

'We have a problem,' said Harry.

'What is it this time?' asked Jake. He was used to Harry being involved in all sorts of strange stuff these days.

'Giant slugs. They're going to try and take over the world.'

'O . . . K . . .' said Jake, wondering if he'd actually woken up yet. 'When you say giant, how big are we actually talking?'

'Well, yesterday I guess they were about the size of a big fat cat. But I think they might be even bigger now.

'So what do you want me to do about it?' Jake asked.

'They're on the allotments next to the school. Granddad and I are going to try and track them down tonight. Maybe you can come along and give us a hand,' said Harry.

'I guess so,' said Jake, and then instantly wished he hadn't.

'Have you heard the news?' said Mum at breakfast. She had the TV on and was listening to a live report. 'There's been a load of vandals down at the allotments. They've made a real mess by the sound of it. Did you and Granddad see anyone last night?'

'Er, no. No people, anyway,' said Harry vaguely, as he gave Ron some muesli.

'I don't know what the world's coming to, really I don't,' Mum said, wiping the cereal off the toy bunny that Daisy had been trying to feed. 'In my day we respected other people's property. If I —'

Harry stopped listening. Mum was starting one of those 'In my day' speeches like all adults do.

He finished his breakfast and turned on the computer. He searched the web, looking for stuff about slugs, and found out loads of fascinating facts. They like the dark, they like damp, they have a really good sense of smell but don't see particularly well, they can devour loads of food and love juicy things

like strawberries, and definitely don't like salt.

Finally he found a link to a video with someone putting salt on a slug, like Granddad had said people do as a last resort to get rid of them.

'Ewwwwwwww! Gross. Look, Ron.'

Ron winced.

'That's really nasty.'

Harry decided it was time to go to Granddad's and tell him about his dream the previous night.

Having heard what they'd been saying on the television, Harry was beginning to think that his dream had come true.

'Mum, I'm going to see if Granddad needs any help at the allotment – you know, with the vandals and everything.'

'OK, Harry, you are a thoughtful boy. I'll let him know you're on your way.'

Harry grabbed Ron and cycled to his granddad's house. Granddad was already waiting outside.

'Morning, Granddad,' he said.

'Morning, Harry. I'm all prepared.' He had a huge carrier bag filled with containers of salt.

'Hmmm,' said Harry. 'I'm not so sure about the salt now. Can you imagine the gunge?'

Granddad thought for a moment. 'I can see what you mean, I suppose. Slugs that size would create a huge amount of gunge. Still, I think I'll take it, just in case.'

'Fair enough,' said Harry as they walked to the allotments, but he really hoped they wouldn't have to use the salt.

Chapter Eight

A Confession

The allotments were filled with angry gardeners trying to clear up the mess left by the slugs. There wasn't very much remaining in the way of vegetables and there certainly wasn't a single strawberry in sight. A really foul smell hung in the air. Fortunately, all of the gardeners were wearing gloves – otherwise their hands would have been stinging like crazy from the slug slime. Harry had brought a pair of his old goalie gloves. He knew they weren't actually for gardening but he liked them much better than Granddad's scratchy spare gardening gloves.

Then Miss Bunsen arrived at the allotments. She looked in horror at her wrecked shed, and at the slime trails that led away from her allotment in every direction.

'Oh no! What have you done?!' she shrieked.

The slugs had eaten every single one of her vegetables.

'All gone! Why oh why did you eat my vegetables, you ungrateful creatures? Boo hoo hoo!'

The other gardeners were beginning to stare. Miss Bunsen was usually such a quiet old lady.

'There, there, my dear,' said Mr Muckerjee, who ran the newsagent's opposite Harry's school. 'It's just vandals. It's happened to all of us – look.'

'No, you don't understand!' she wailed. She

was crawling around on the ground now, despite the stinging slime, searching for just one uneaten vegetable. 'They've escaped, they're gone, all of them. Who knows what will happen now? Oh, what have I done?!'

'Er, well, I don't think this is your fault, Miss Bunsen,' said Mr Muckerjee, starting to worry about her strange behaviour. Why don't you sit down and have a nice cup of tea?'

'So it was you,' said Harry quietly. 'I thought so.'

BOO HOO HOO.
MY LOVELY
VEGETABLES!

He and Granddad exchanged glances. Miss Bunsen turned her tear-stained face towards them, and burst into tears again.

'Come along now, Miss Bunsen,' said Granddad. 'Let's get you that cup of tea and have a little chat. Thank you, Mr Muckerjee, we'll take it from here.'

Mr Muckerjee happily walked away, relieved not to have to look after her.

They led Miss Bunsen over to Granddad's

little shed and sat her down. Granddad put the bag full of salt in the corner.

'Here,' said Granddad, giving her a hanky to wipe her face. 'I think you'd better tell us all about it.'

So, Dotty Bunsen told them all about her disappointments with the Giant Vegetable Competition and her plan to get the giant slugs to eat Granddad's marrows.

'But I never meant for this to happen!' she sighed.

'My marrows!' said Granddad. 'I haven't even checked on them.' He ran out of the shed and headed to his greenhouse.

'So what happened last night?' asked Harry.

'They must have broken out of their cage, and —' Miss Bunsen stopped and looked guiltily at Harry, her eyes brimming with tears.

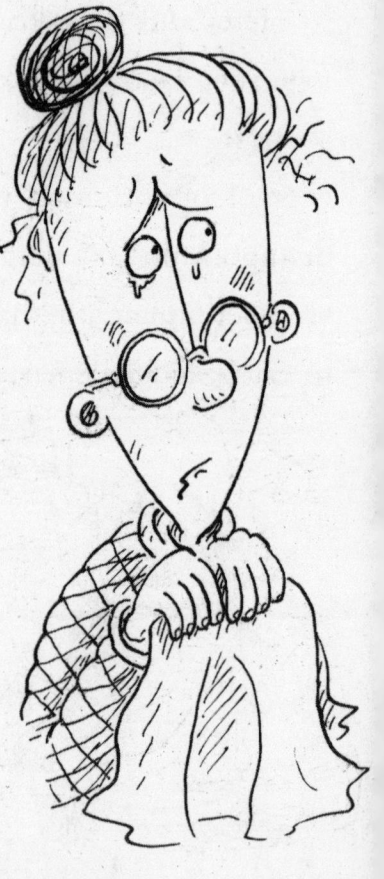

'What is it?' he said.

'Erm . . . I think they've eaten the rest of my Super-Grow,' she mumbled.

Harry's nightmare from the night before flashed into his mind. It definitely seemed that it wasn't just a nightmare. 'Now they've escaped,' she went on, 'what if they breed? They were big before but if they've eaten all that Super-Grow . . . The world could be filled with giant slugs! I think they're getting cleverer too, the more they grow. They obviously worked out how to get out of the shed. They'll devour everything and it will all be my fault. Oh what have I done?' She started crying again.

'Stop that,' said Harry, getting a bit annoyed. 'Crying's no good to us. We need you to help us work out what we can do to stop the slimy menaces.'

Granddad came back from the greenhouse.

'Phew,' he said. 'Margaret . . .' He blushed. '. . . I mean, the marrows, are all safe.'

Miss Bunsen looked at him, her face filled with shame. 'I'm so sorry,' she said. 'Jealousy is a terrible thing.'

'Right,' said Harry. 'Let's work out what to do. Is there anything you can tell us that might help?'

'Well you won't be able to do anything until it's dark,' said Miss Bunsen. 'The slugs won't come out in the day time – they hate the light. They seem to have become super-sensitive since I started giving them the compound. The biggest was about half a metre tall yesterday, but with all the

Super-Grow it will be bigger than that now.'

'So we'll have to come back tonight then,' said Harry.

'And use the salt!' said Granddad. 'I told you, that's the answer.'

'*No!*' said Miss Bunsen. 'You can't – that would be murder!'

'But they're only slugs,' said Granddad, astonished.

'Slugs have feelings too, and mine are special.

They all have their own personalities.'

Harry found that a little hard to believe, but he remembered what an animal lover Miss Bunsen was. And Granddad said that talking to his marrows made them grow, and he was a champion marrow grower. Anything seemed possible at that moment.

'OK, calm down,' said Harry. 'We have to

PEAT FREE COMPOST

capture them before they can do any more damage. But we don't know where they are.'

'Maybe I could try and make a shrinking powder and bring them back to normal size,' suggested Miss Bunsen, cheering up a little.'

'It would take a while to work though, surely, and what would we do with them in the meantime?' asked Harry.

'Perhaps we could trap them somehow?' said Granddad.

'Yes, it's "How" that's the problem,' said Harry. 'They must still be on the allotments though, because the fence isn't broken. But they won't want to stay here much longer since they've nearly run out of food. We'll just have to come back later and play it by ear. Miss Bunsen, you get to work on that shrinking powder – it's worth a try.'

'Absolutely.' She nodded enthusiastically.

'And we'll all meet back here tonight at dusk,' said Harry.

There was something else worrying Harry though. The nearest source of vegetables to the allotments was the school Gardening Club plot, and Harry knew there was something growing there that they found irresistible. Strawberries. But the only way to get to it was straight across the football pitch . . . Harry shivered at the thought of a slug-slimed pitch.

This was definitely a job for Super Soccer Boy.

Chapter Nine

Slug Alert

When Harry got home, Mum was just about to go to the supermarket with Daisy.

'Mum,' said Harry angelically, 'I need something for an experiment at school. Can you get me some cooking salt while you're out?' Harry had seen big bags of cooking salt in the supermarket before and thought they'd be ideal.

'What sort of experiment?' asked Mum,

always keen to encourage Harry with his work.

'Oh, erm, just something to do with the Gardening Club.' Well, it was almost the truth. He doubted she'd believe the real truth. 'Two kilos should just about do it.'

'How much?!' said Mum. 'Well, I suppose if it's for school . . . At least it's not expensive. OK, I'll get it while I'm out. Come on, Daisy.'

'Thanks, Mum,' said Harry.

He spent the rest of the afternoon working on some ideas of how to trap the slugs.

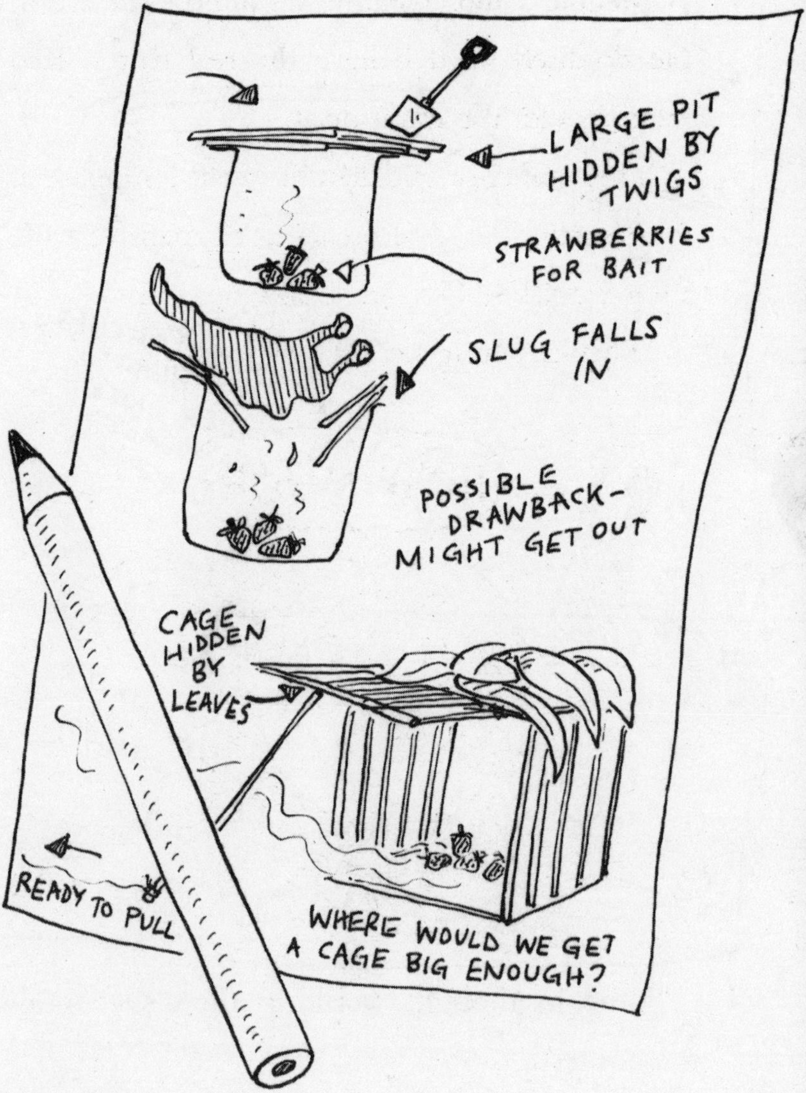

LARGE PIT HIDDEN BY TWIGS

STRAWBERRIES FOR BAIT

SLUG FALLS IN

POSSIBLE DRAWBACK— MIGHT GET OUT

CAGE HIDDEN BY LEAVES

READY TO PULL

WHERE WOULD WE GET A CAGE BIG ENOUGH?

Some, he thought, would be more successful
than others.

Jake arrived at his house just after dinner.

'Evening, Harry. I thought these might come in handy.' He'd brought a couple of fishing nets – the kind that you buy at the seaside to look at the stuff in rockpools. 'So what's the plan?'

'I'll tell you on the way,' said Harry. 'It's getting dark so we'd better go. Here, take this.' He handed Jake a backpack – it was very heavy. 'It's mostly in case of an emergency.'

Jake looked inside. 'It's a water gun!' said Jake. 'Are we going to have a water fight?' he asked excitedly. 'Isn't it a bit cold for that?'

'Don't be daft,' said Harry. 'It's for the slugs. It's filled with salt water in case they get out of control. I've attached it to a tank that you wear on your back so you don't have to keep refilling it.'

'Cool!' said Jake. 'I'll be a Ghostbuster.'

'Slugbuster more like,' Harry said with a laugh.

Harry picked up a big, bulky backpack of his own and Ron climbed on top.

'These slugs,' said Jake. 'They're not dangerous, are they?'

'About as dangerous as an enormous slug could be I suppose,' said Harry.

'That's not very reassuring,' said Jake.

They got on their bikes and rode to the allotments.

'Poo! Is that you Harry?' asked Jake. 'What did you have for dinner?'

'It's the slug slime,' answered Harry. 'It stinks. It stings your hands too, so be careful. I've got my goalie gloves – I put my spare ones in the backpack for you.'

As usual, Jake was beginning to wish that he hadn't come. He felt like he was walking into a vampire or werewolf movie.

By the time they reached the allotments, the sun had almost set. Granddad and Miss Bunsen were already there waiting.

'At last!' said Granddad. 'Miss Bunsen was just telling me she's made a good start on the shrinking powder.'

'A good *start*?' Harry said.

'Well,' she explained, 'the trouble is it will have to be done in several stages. It took me years to develop my Super-Grow and to begin with it

wasn't very strong. It's the same with this shrinking compound. It's only a weak formula at the moment. It could take weeks, even months, to get the slugs back to normal size.'

'That's if we can catch them,' said Granddad.

'Once they're back to their normal size, will they go back to their normal behaviour or will we just have normal-sized crazy slugs roaming the country?' asked Harry.

'Oh I couldn't let them go. Who knows what trouble they might get into?' said Mrs Bunsen. 'I'll have to keep them and look after them. After all, it's my fault they're like they are. I can keep them safe and comfortable at home with me.'

'OK, good,' said Jake, not feeling at all reassured. He couldn't believe they were having a conversation about mutant slugs.

'But where are we going to put them when we've caught them?' asked Harry. 'I've thought of that too,' said Miss Bunsen. 'We can keep them in my garage. There's plenty of room because I never park my car in it.

It's nice and dark and it has a big up-and-over door. It's not far either – the driveway goes down the back of the houses on the other side of the playing field. My garage is the one at the end.'

Harry took out his notepad and drew a map.

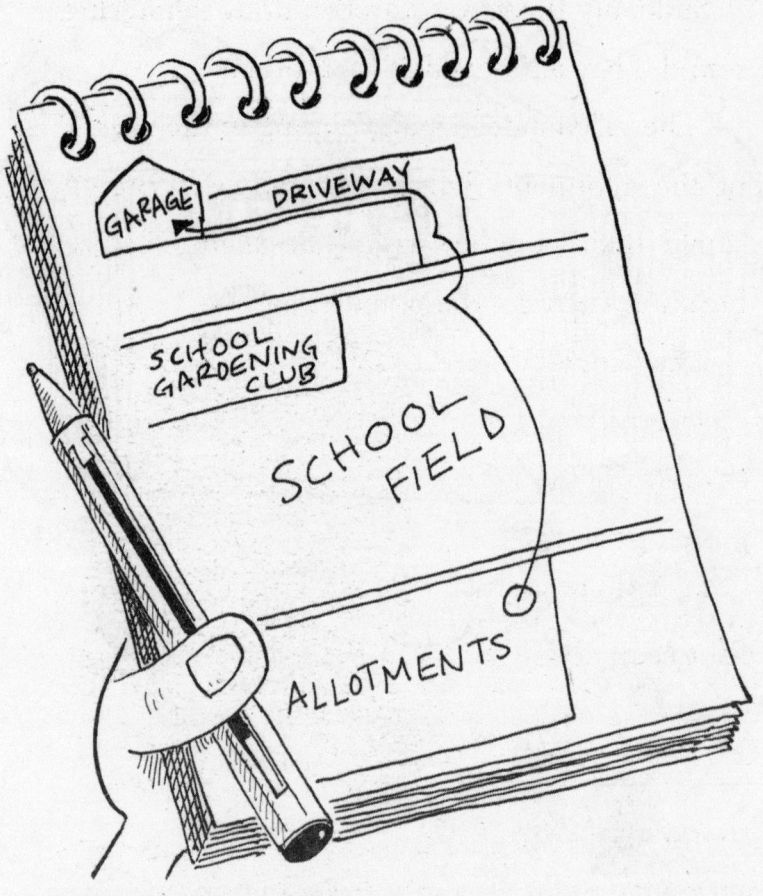

He didn't feel happy that the slugs would have to cross the football pitch. Not at all!

'OK,' he said, reluctantly. 'So after we have them cornered, we have to get them over there. I think I know how —'

Suddenly there was a tremendous splintering sound. They all looked at each other.

'There!' Granddad said, pointing to the corner of the allotments where Mr and Mrs Brown stored their potatoes in a large shed. 'They're breaking in to get the potatoes!'

They could all see an enormous shadowy figure glistening in the semi-dark. It was at least two metres long!

For a moment everyone was speechless.

Jake looked at the nets he'd brought. 'I don't think these are going to do it

somehow,' he said eventually, with a glazed
expression on his face.

'What about your marrows, Granddad?' said
Harry. 'What if they break into the greenhouse?'

'I put a thick line of salt all the way around. If
they try and get past that they'll get a shock.'

Miss Bunsen gasped and went a little pale.

'I'm sorry,' said Granddad, 'but if it's them or
my marrows, I'm afraid it's no contest. My
marrows will always come first.'

More splintering sounds came from another part of the allotments.

'The seed store,' said Miss Bunsen.

They stood listening to the eerie sounds of splintering and slurping going on around them. Harry, with super fast speed and accuracy, shone his torch around the allotments, counting the slugs before they had time to slink away into the shadows.

'I can only see nine,' he said. 'You said there were ten.'

Crunch!!

'Sounds like we've found the tenth,' shouted Jake.

They all caught sight of the slimy black creature as Harry flashed the torch in its direction. It was over by the fence, which separated the allotments from the playing field.

'I d–d–don't believe it!' said Jake. 'It's huge!'

He wasn't wrong.

'It's the biggest of the lot,' said Harry.

Just then, the clouds moved away from the moon and they could all see the giant slugs, spread from one side of the allotments to the other. They were surrounded.

The biggest slug stopped for a moment and swayed from side to side. Instantly, the others stopped what they were doing and swayed from side to side too. Then they started to move towards the biggest slug.

'They're communicating with each other!' said Harry.

There was something incredible about the shiny, slimy creatures. Their sheer size was extraordinary.

Harry gasped in horror. It was a really scary sight.

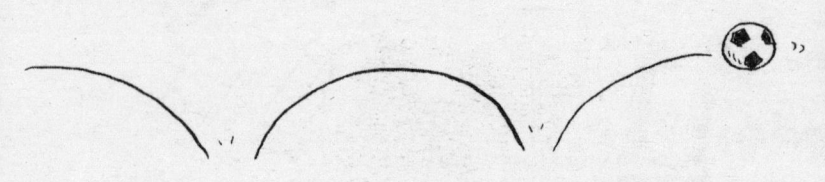

Chapter Ten

Football Patch

Harry hoped his plan would still work, even though the slugs were far bigger than he'd feared. He thought he'd be able to lure the slugs to Miss Bunsen's garage – his main worries were that the slugs would ruin the football pitch on the way, and that he might not have enough salt to keep them there.

They all watched in amazement as the rest of the slugs moved across the allotments to the big slug by the fence that seemed to be their leader. Then, as one, the slugs joined together to push at the fence to the playing fields.

'Surely they won't be able to break that down?' said Jake. 'It's chain link — it's really strong.'

'But look at the size of them, Jake!' said Granddad, shaking. 'All that weight! I don't see how it's going to hold.'

They were rocking the fence backwards and forwards now. Each time it moved a little more.

'Why that fence, though?' said Miss Bunsen. 'Why not just go for the gate? It would be much easier.'

'The school Gardening Club has a vegetable patch. I'll bet that's what they're after – they've got an amazing sense of smell,' said Harry.

'Are there strawberries growing there?' asked Miss Bunsen.

'Yes,' said Jake. 'They're everybody's favourite.'

'And that includes slugs,' said Miss Bunsen. 'If they can smell the strawberries, it'll drive them crazy.'

At that moment, there was a crash and the fence gave way completely. The slugs poured

onto the playing field, spreading out as they crossed it.

'No!' said Jake. 'Not the Gardening Club patch! I've got a pumpkin growing there for Halloween.'

'Never mind that – look what they're doing to the football pitch!' yelled Harry. 'Jake, get the water gun ready – we may need it. Follow me, everybody!'

Harry raced at super speed, using his finest footwork to glide through the allotments, dodging the garden poles, darting between the ruined piles of vegetables and stinging slime, and leaping over pots and piles of compost. When he

reached the fence, the slugs were already halfway across the football pitch, their foul trails scorching the grass as they went. Harry tried not to think about it and reached for his torch.

'I'll stop you, you slimy slugs!' he roared, switching on the torch. He shone it right in the face of the nearest slug and it shrank away with a weird squelchy, squeaky sound, and changed direction away from the light.

Harry darted around the slugs, skilfully shining the torch from side to side until he managed to direct them the way he wanted them to go. He zoomed this way and that – he was almost invisible he was going at such a speed – until he had herded them all up.

'What now?' he said to himself, continuing to circle round the slugs to keep them from moving away. 'I can't keep this up forever.'

Then he spotted the football goal – and the goal nets. 'Perfect!' he said.

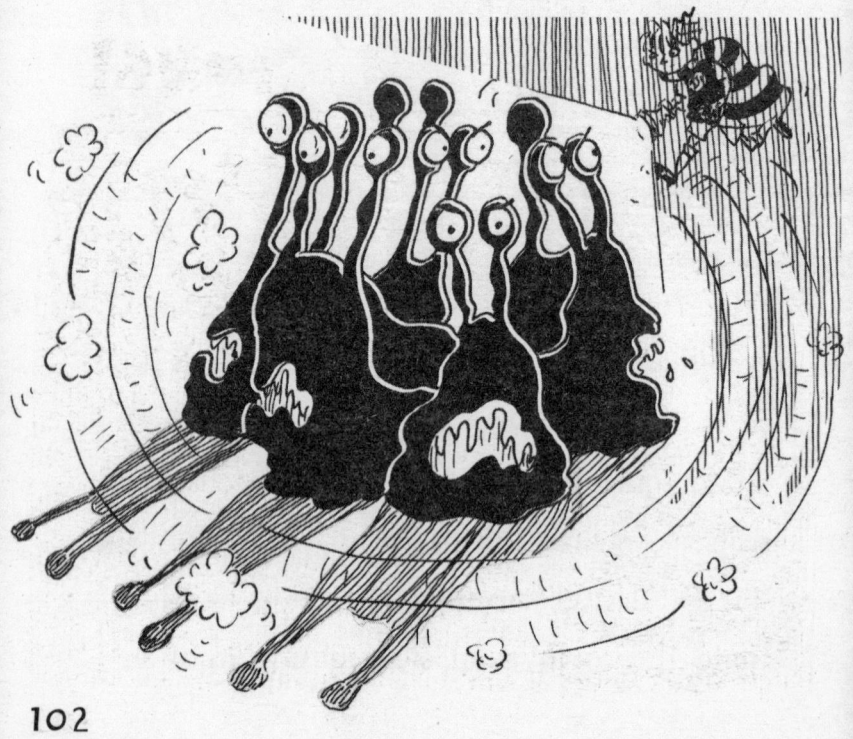

Harry forced the slugs to move towards the mouth of the goal. The slugs were ruining the grass, but at least the goal mouth was the muddiest part of the pitch – there actually wasn't that much grass there left to ruin.

'Harry! Harry!' shouted Jake as he caught up. 'What are you doing?'

'I'm slug herding!' said Harry, feeling like a shepherd. 'I'm getting them into the goal. Stand by with the water gun.'

When Granddad and Miss Bunsen arrived on the scene, Harry had managed to herd all of the slugs into the goal and was shining the torch on them to keep them in place. Jake stood behind with the water gun to stop them trying to escape out of the back. The combined strength of the slugs could easily break the net, but a couple of squirts with the gun had been enough to show

that Jake meant business – as soon as they sensed the salty water they knew how dangerous the odd-looking gun actually was. If you were a slug that is. It wasn't a particularly strong solution of salt but it certainly must have stung them a bit.

'Stay back, you slimy monsters,' shouted Jake, suddenly feeling very brave. 'You're not getting my pumpkin!'

'So now what?' puffed Granddad, out of breath from the run. He shone his torch at the cowering slugs, too.

Miss Bunsen looked at the captives and felt a huge pang of guilt. She wondered how she'd let everything get so out of control.

'Now,' said Harry, 'all we have to do is get this lot to the garage.' He handed his torch to Miss Bunsen. You and Granddad keep them pinned down with the torches. I'll be back as soon as I can with the next step of 'Operation Slug Shift'.'

What no one realised was that the slug slime was beginning to eat away at the net . . .

Chapter Eleven

Salty Footballs

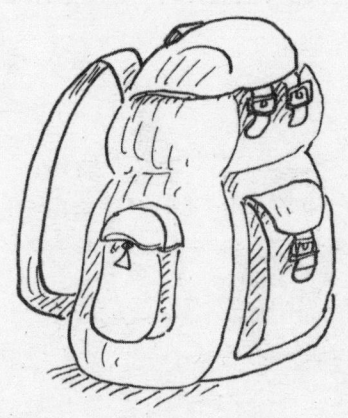

Harry whizzed back to Granddad's allotment and got his backpack.

'OK,' he said to Ron, who'd been waiting patiently in the shed. 'I need some of Granddad's garden twine.'

While Harry was busy outside, Ron climbed the shelves in Granddad's shed until he found the twine. He pushed it off onto the floor and rolled it outside to Harry.

'Thanks, Ron.'

Harry had gathered together a load of bamboo poles from around the allotments and he strung them together with the garden twine to make one long pole.

'OK, now for the salt carriers,' he said. Out of the bulky backpack, he took four old footballs and the bags of cooking salt he'd conned his Mum into buying earlier on. On the side of each football, there was a hole about the size of a pound coin, stuffed with a cork. On the other side was a bigger hole. They had string already attached.

'Pass me the funnel out of the bag, Ron. I wish I'd had time to do this before we left,' he said, looking at the angry slugs, trapped in the goal net.

Putting the funnel in the hole at the top of each of the footballs, Harry filled them with salt.

'OK, nearly ready.' He put everything, including Ron, into a wheelbarrow. Then he quickly whizzed around gathering up as much uneaten veg as he could. There wasn't a lot. 'Let's go!'

'I'm so glad you're here,' said Granddad when Harry got back to the goal. 'The slugs are getting very restless. They must be desperate for those strawberries in the school vegetable patch. I hope you know what you're doing.'

'Here's the plan,' said Harry as he unloaded the wheelbarrow and finished constructing his giant salt-shaker. The slugs had already spotted the food in the wheelbarrow and were straining towards it. 'We have to get the slugs to Miss Bunsen's garage over there.

That means
we have to
guide them
without losing any
on the way. That's
where this comes in.'

Harry held up his contraption. 'This will create a path they have to stick to or they'll end up as goo. They know only too well what happens to them if they touch salt.'

'Clever!' said Jake.

'Granddad, you and Miss Bunsen will drop food out of the wheelbarrow to tempt them forwards, the way we want them to go. Jake will follow on behind with the water gun.'

'Brilliant, Harry,' said his granddad, impressed.

'There is just one thing, Granddad . . .'

'Yes, Harry, what is it?'

'We may need to use one of your marrows.'

'My m-m-marrows!' Granddad said sadly.

'We have to get the slugs through the fence. It'll need something really tempting to do that. If they see one of your giant marrows, they're so greedy it might just do the trick and they'll break through to get at it.'

Granddad gulped. 'I suppose if you put it like that. But not Margaret, though. Please let me save her.'

'Of course, Granddad.'

Miss Bunsen touched his arm gently. She understood what a sacrifice he was making.

'Er . . . Harry!' shouted Jake with a bit of a wobble in his voice 'You'd better get a move on – the net is rotting.'

Suddenly the slugs burst out of the back of the net and it took some furious squirting of the salty water to make them turn around.

'Good work, Jake, keep them moving this

way. Right, if everybody's ready,' said Harry, 'I'll start the path. You lure them along it, then I'll go back for the bait. Let's go!'

Harry pulled the corks out of the first two footballs and a steady stream of salt fell in two lines about ten metres apart. He tried not to think about the damage the salt and the slugs were doing to the football pitch.

'OK, point the torches away and start dropping the food. If you run out, I'll have to grab some from the school garden. Don't worry, Jake, I won't touch the pumpkins.'

They did as Harry instructed and the slugs moved in an orderly line, munching up the veg. By the time Harry reached the fence, the first two footballs were almost empty.

'Chocks away,' he said, pulling out the second set of corks. He pressed the hover button on the controls of his

Utility Boots – his best invention so far – and flew over the fence and on down the driveway until he'd reached Miss Bunsen's garage. But when he looked back he realised that the salt trails ran out about five metres before the garage.

'Oh dear,' he said, 'I was hoping that wouldn't happen. Nothing I can do about it now though.'

Harry rushed back to the others. He arrived just in time.

'Harry! Quick!' said Granddad. 'They're going to slime us!'

He and Miss Bunsen were running along, with the slugs in hot pursuit. Ron was hanging onto

the handle of the wheelbarrow for dear life.

'Keep going!' called Harry as he flew past and into the Gardening Club veggy patch. He grabbed a couple of juicy-looking tomato plants and some beans (he wasn't fond of beans). Then, as much as he loved them himself, he grabbed a load of strawberries as well. He whizzed back, dropping them in the wheelbarrow as he passed. 'I'm going to get the marrow,' he said. 'I'll be back.'

Harry pressed the Turbo button on the controls of his Utility Boots, which gave him real super speed – even by Super Soccer Boy standards! Almost immediately, he was back at Granddad's greenhouse, picking out the second largest marrow. He thought it was the one Granddad had called Marie but he wasn't sure.

'Wow! This is heavy!' he groaned as he picked it up. Just in time, he spotted the bag filled with the tubs of salt that Granddad had left there earlier, and grabbed that too. Then he jetted back to the playing field where Granddad was just beginning to run out of strawberries. The slugs were nearly at the fence now so Harry flew over and hovered on the other side of it.

'Granddad, grab the wheelbarrow and move away,' shouted Harry. 'I'll take it from here.' He waved the giant marrow in the air. 'Ooooo, sluggies! Look what I've got for you! A nice, big, juicy, giant marrow! It smells amazing. Come and get it,' he said temptingly.

COME AND GET IT!

You should have seen the look on their faces! The slugs headed straight for the fence, sliming along at top speed and, as Harry had predicted, it instantly splintered beneath them.

'Hooray!' cheered Jake, happy too that his pumpkin would live to see Halloween. Granddad and Miss Bunsen were just relieved that they were no longer being chased.

The slugs followed Harry greedily towards Miss Bunsen's open garage. But when the salty path started to get thinner, the big slug at the front began to veer off, turning towards the garden next door where it had obviously smelled something yummy.

'Oh no you don't!' said Harry. 'Hey you! Slime face! This way!'

In desperation, Harry launched the marrow towards the garage with one super kick. It hit the back wall and exploded all over the walls. None of the slugs couldn't resist the juicy bits of marrow splattered everywhere and all of them sped to the garage to devour it. As soon as the last one was inside, Harry pulled the door down behind them.

'Phew!' said Granddad as he and the others joined Harry at the door. 'I'm glad that's over.'

'It's not over yet,' said Harry as he lifted Ron out of the wheelbarrow. 'Not until Miss Bunsen has shrunk them back to normal size.'

'Come inside for a cup of cocoa – I think we've all earned it,' said Miss Bunsen. 'And then

I can show you how far I've got with the shrinking compound.'

They could hear the slugs thrashing around inside the garage.

'Shouldn't we make sure they can't get out?' said Jake. 'I mean, if they can break down fences . . .'

'Good point, Jake,' said Granddad. 'We could sprinkle some salt around or something.'

'I guess it would be best to be on the safe side,' said Harry.

They sprinkled all the salt from Granddad's bag onto the ground in front of the garage door.

'There, that should do it,' said Harry.

Chapter Twelve

Greed

Harry tried not to worry about how on earth they would find enough food to keep feeding the imprisoned giant slugs. It was going to be hard to hide them for long.

Miss Bunsen made everybody a steaming mug of cocoa. Before he'd even started his cocoa, Granddad fell asleep and was snoring gently in front of the TV.

'So, Miss Bunsen, do you have any idea how long it's going to take you to get them back to normal?' asked Harry.

'Let me show you how far I've got. You see,' she said, 'I've been working on the principle that a slug's body is roughly seventy per cent water so I —'

Miss Bunsen's explanation was cut short by a crashing, crunching noise from outside.

'I don't like the sound of that,' said Harry.

The crunching was followed by what sounded very much like a metal garage door being ripped off its frame. Granddad woke with a start.

'What the —?' He'd been having a strange dream about giant slugs, or that's what he thought, until he saw where he was and remembered it had actually happened.

They all looked at each other.

'The slugs are escaping. Quick! Grab the torches and the water gun,' said Harry.

Then there was an ear-splitting scream. Well, not exactly a scream, more a slimy squeak – after all, slugs have no vocal cords.

Harry and his helpers ran outside and headed for the driveway. Harry, of course, got there first.

'Guys,' he said quietly, 'I don't think we're going to need the torches – or the water gun.'

'Oh no!' said Miss Bunsen. 'You silly greedy things.'

'Poo!' said Granddad.

There was a bubbling, gooey, stinky mess of disintegrating slugs all over the driveway.

PONG!

There was so much goo, it had spread all the way across, seeping through the gaps in fences and scorching the weeds.

'That is truly gross,' said Jake. 'What a pong!'

'Looks like they were trying to get to the neighbour's garden,' said Granddad.

'It does, doesn't it? I expect they could smell strawberries,' said Harry.

'That's what they would have been after then,' said Miss Bunsen with a sniff.

'Killed by their own greedy appetites,' said Harry. 'Come on, I think we're going to need a hose.'

Chapter Thirteen

Post-Match Analysis

Three weeks later, Harry's granddad once again won the Giant Vegetable Competition (Marrow Section) – with Margaret, of course. Not only that but, as he'd hoped, he also won Best in Show. But then he didn't have any competition from the other gardeners on the allotments – all their vegetables had been eaten! He and Miss Bunsen were good friends now. They had exchanged lots of gardening tips and Granddad had even offered to give her some of his special marrow seeds.

Nobody else ever heard about the giant slugs. There was no actual evidence that they'd ever existed. The school Gardening Club were upset that some of their plants had gone but Jake could hardly tell them what had really happened. It wasn't completely disastrous though – there were still pumpkins for Halloween. All of the mess was put down to vandals, but who the vandals were remained a mystery to everyone. Well, everyone but Harry, Granddad, Jake and Miss Bunsen.

As for the football pitch, it had been completely wrecked. But with a few packets of grass seed and a sprinkling of Miss Bunsen's Super-Grow, all of the bare patches soon began to recover. Miss Bunsen even promised Harry that she would look after the pitch and keep it in top condition to make up for all the trouble she'd caused. It wasn't long before it was the best football pitch in the district.

That made Harry very happy!

HARRY'S F⚽OTBALL FACTS!

The first international football match was played on 30th Nov 1872 between England + Scotland.

Everton FC's nickname is 'The toffees'

In 2002 the FA said that 61,667 women and girls were playing competitive football.

In the 2006 World Cup, Thierry Henry committed 20 fouls. The most by any player!

In 1995 a Man City fan was banned from taking dead chickens into the ground.

He used to swing them around his head if City scored!

Early football boots had the studs nailed in with a hammer.

Referees originally signalled decisions by waving a hanky.

The tallest current football player, is Belgian goalkeeper Kristof von Hout at 2.08m (6ft 10in)

The shortest is Brazilian Élton Jose Xavier Gomes at 1.58m (5ft 2in)

Join
Super Soccer Boy
online:

www.supersoccerboy.com

⚽Fun activities
⚽Football facts and quiz
⚽All the latest on the books
And much more!

Go to
www.piccadillypress.co.uk
to find more books
you'll love!